Jack Creek Cowboy
by Neil Johnson

 Dial Books for Young Readers / New York

Special thanks to Bill Gentle, Deputy Commissioner of the Wyoming Department of Agriculture, for checking the facts in this book.

Published by Dial Books for Young Readers
A Division of Penguin Books USA Inc.
375 Hudson Street
New York, New York 10014

Design by Nancy R. Leo
Printed in Hong Kong
by South China Printing Company (1988) Limited
First Edition
10 9 8 7 6 5 4 3 2 1

Library of Congress Cataloging in Publication Data

Johnson, Neil, 1954–
Jack Creek cowboy / by Neil Johnson.
p.   cm.
Summary: Text and photographs follow ten-year-old Justin Whitlock through the summer when he and his older brother Corey helped their father with an important cowboy job on their Wyoming ranch.
ISBN 0-8037-1228-6 (trade). — ISBN 0-8037-1229-4 (lib. bdg.)
1. Ranch life — Wyoming — Juvenile literature.
2. Cowboys — Wyoming — Juvenile literature.
3. Wyoming — Social life and customs — Juvenile literature.
[1. Ranch life.   2. Cowboys.   3. Wyoming — Social life and customs.]
I. Title.
F761.J64 1993   978.7'009734 — dc20   92-921   CIP   AC r92

To Jonathan,
quesadillas on the patio,
and picture-perfect boomerang returns.

The herds of buffalo are gone from the valley of the Greybull River in northwest Wyoming. The Shoshone and Mountain Crow people who once lived here and hunted the buffalo are also gone. Today the only relics of their hunting parties are the stone spearheads and arrowheads that are still found by those with sharp eyes and the patience to look for them.

For over one hundred years now, the Pitchfork Ranch has stretched across the Greybull Valley in the shadow of Francs Peak—named for Otto Franc, the man who founded the ranch in 1878 and first climbed the tall mountain. The Pitchfork raises and sells cattle for beef.

Francs Peak is on the edge of the Absaroka Mountain range, part of the Rocky Mountains. Back in Otto Franc's time, herds of cattle grazed the plentiful grass of the valley during the spring. In the summer they were moved up into the mountain meadows near Francs Peak for the rich summer grass, and were brought back down to feed on harvested hay during the fall and winter. Cowboys on horseback worked long, hard hours in conditions ranging from the blazing summer sun to blinding winter snows.

A rancher named Louis G. Phelps bought the Pitchfork after Franc died in 1903, and today the ranch is still owned and run by Phelps's descendants. There are fewer ranch hands and more machines and vehicles to help the hands do the hard work and to get around. New barns are made of metal, not wood. There are more fences, better ranching methods, better land conservation methods, and even better breeds of cattle than there were in Otto Franc's day.

But even though the Pitchfork needs fewer hands to work it, the basic jobs remain very much the same as they did a century ago. These jobs are usually done by grown men and women. But one summer a ten-year-old boy living on the Pitchfork Ranch and his older brother helped their father with an important cowboy job for the first time.

On the last day of school the bus lets Justin Whitlock out near the cattle barn just down the dirt road from his home. He lives on the Pitchfork Ranch, where his father, Scott, is one of the hands.

Because the ranch is a good distance from town, Justin, who's ten, won't be seeing much of his nineteen classmates during the summer. But he and his twelve-year-old brother, Corey, will be busy riding, looking for arrowheads, raising pigs for their 4-H projects, playing in the barns, watching for wild animals—and helping their father with a special job. This summer Scott Whitlock has promised to take his boys into the mountains with him when it's time to work the cattle up on summer range.

The trip to the mountains isn't until the end of July. For now the boys are eager to explore the woods, hills, pastures, and prairie around the huge ranch, something there isn't much time to do during the school year. They must do their exploring on foot, not horseback. They can duck under the barbed wire fences, but neither of them is strong enough yet to open and shut the tightly stretched fence gates to let a horse pass through.

The cattle that roam the Pitchfork range share the grass with deer and antelope, who easily jump over or crawl under the fences. May and June is the time to watch for the wild animals' newborn babies. "I'll be walking along and a baby antelope will jump up and scare the hoot owl out of me!" says Justin. The

dogs build their unwelcome "villages" in the middle of pastures, where horses or cattle might step into one of the many prairie dog holes and break a leg.

Justin and Corey help out at home in the summertime, but they haven't done much ranch work before this summer. Most of the work must be done by skilled hands like their father, Scott.

———

Scott Whitlock can fix a truck engine and work the irrigation system, but the cowboy part of the job is his favorite. He and the boys' mother, Sheila, both grew up on and around ranches. To them, living in a big city would be like living in a foreign country.

Lee, Stephanie, Joe, and Louis are some of the

little babies look just like the many rocks in the prairie when they are curled up tightly on the ground.

Out on the prairie Justin and Corey see an antelope chasing a bald eagle. The hungry eagle has spotted a baby antelope, but whenever the eagle swoops in close, the mother threatens the low-flying bird with her sharp hoofs. The boys also get a close look at a fawn lying in the long grass. The mother deer watches from nearby as the boys move on quickly and quietly.

There are plenty of other animals around. A fox raises her four cubs right beside one of the ranch roads, and beaver build dams across two of the streams flowing into the Greybull River. One dam is not too far from the ranch buildings. Pesky prairie

other employees on the Pitchfork. Like Scott, they also enjoy working with the cattle from horseback— but as professional ranch hands, they have many other jobs. In running a cattle ranch there is hay to irrigate and harvest. There are irrigation ditches to be dug or cleaned out. There are pickup trucks and many other machines that constantly need fixing. There are always fences to repair. With all the year-round work to do, there are some other hands who never even get on a horse.

Even though many of the ranch hands on the Pitchfork can ride, rope, and work cattle, Ray is the only year-round cowboy on the ranch. Ray is the cattle foreman, and working with the cattle is his only job. He hates machines and he says machines hate him.

Sometimes one of the horses needs to be reshod. In the barn, Ray grabs hold of the horse's leg and raises the hoof up between his knees, scolding the huge animal when it tries to move. He pries off the horseshoe, cleans and trims the hoof, and then puts the shoe back on, hammering in shiny new nails. Taking good care of the ranch horses is very important because cattle can only be worked from horseback.

Early each morning a ranch hand drives a pickup out into the horse pasture on the hills above Justin's home and honks the horn. At the sound of the horn all the ranch horses come running down the hill to the corral beside the horse barn.

They thunder down the dirt road, kicking up a cloud of dust. They are ready for a breakfast of oats and another day's work. Brewster, the ranch horse Justin rides, is among them.

Scott and Sheila moved to the Pitchfork when Justin was only two. As a little boy he didn't even want to go near a horse or a cow. Later his father put him on a horse for short periods of time. Justin remembers how his legs stuck straight out from the saddle. It was very scary being so high up on such a powerful animal, and Justin would only ride for a few minutes at a time.

But as he grew older, his legs grew longer. He found that once his feet fit properly into the stirrups of the saddle, he could ride for longer periods of time. Now he can ride for hours as long as the horse doesn't go too fast. He's not scared anymore and likes sitting way up above the ground, even higher than the biggest bull.

Still, Scott thinks both Justin and Corey need more experience on horseback before their trip to the mountains. Ray agrees. He has watched these boys grow up and isn't entirely comfortable yet seeing them around the horses and cattle. The animals are extremely strong, and can be very dangerous if they get scared or defensive. A horse once kicked Ray and almost killed him.

So their father takes Justin and Corey out riding whenever he can and teaches them the many skills cowboys need—how to care for a horse, how to ride a long way, how to rope a calf.

The boys practice roping in their yard. First they practice on a fence post. Then one pretends to be the running calf while the other chases him, swinging the rope around and around before throwing it. Justin's loop lands around Corey's ankles and he pulls the rope tight. "I need to learn how to do this from a horse," he says.

One evening everyone goes into town to watch cowboys and cowgirls practice for a roping contest. Justin watches how each rider and horse work closely as a team to see how fast they can rope and stop a small steer running at breakneck speed. Sometimes one rider breaks out of the gate chasing the steer. Other times two riders rope it, one aiming for the head, the other aiming for the hind feet. If a rope misses, the rider must get back in line and await another turn with another steer.

It is important to know how to secure an animal quickly and safely because each spring all the cows with new calves are rounded up for branding. By law each ranch has its own special brand, a burn mark on the hide, to identify an animal's owner all its life. One by one, each calf is roped away from its mother and branded.

At each ranch it is best to do all the calves in one day so that none are missed. The Pitchfork branded about fourteen hundred calves this past spring. Because it was such a big job, neighbors came to help. Wrestling calves to the ground all day long is hard and dirty work.

Fred and Kay, neighboring ranchers, helped with the Pitchfork branding, and now the Whitlocks go down to their ranch to help them brand their calves. Fred ropes each calf from his horse and brings it to Trinity, his daughter, and Justin. They wrestle down

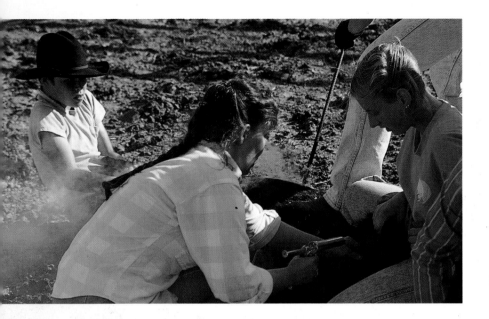

the kicking animal so that it can be branded quickly by Kay. At the same time, Sheila Whitlock gives each calf a shot of medicine with a vaccine gun to protect it from disease.

This may be the only time in the calf's life that it is roped and held down like this. The calf is afraid, but it is quickly back with its mother and the brand only hurts for a short time. After the branding everyone gathers for a big dinner.

After work one afternoon Scott saddles up the horses and takes his sons out riding. Justin loves to ride, but he can remember a time when he lost control of Brewster. The horse began to gallop faster and faster, and all Justin could do to keep from falling was to hold on tightly. He was very scared. Finally he managed to grasp the reins and pull back with all his might. Brewster stopped.

"Never *ever* let your horse take away control from you," Scott reminds Justin now. "The rider should always be the boss. If you are ever chasing a calf and you start to lose control, forget about the calf and stop your horse immediately! Remember, he can run faster than you can ride."

Justin learns to communicate with his horse through the reins that go to the bit in Brewster's mouth, through the spurs on his boots, through his voice, and even through his leg and body movements. The longer Justin rides Brewster, the better Brewster learns to follow Justin's different messages. Justin learns that each horse has a different personality, just as people do. Some are cranky, others are friendly. Some get tired quickly, while others are full of energy. Justin and Brewster learn from each other.

Brewster is an experienced cowhorse, a little slow with age, but Justin likes him because he is honest and dependable.

Justin also learns about the clothes of a cowboy. His wide-brimmed hat provides important protection from the sun, rain, and wind, and adds warmth in the winter. Leather gloves protect his hands. Boots with heels help keep his feet from slipping in the stirrups, and their strong leather protects his feet from cactus and rocks while he is walking. Long leather chaps (or the shorter chinks) protect his legs from the constant rubbing on the saddle and prevent branches from poking him while he's riding through trees or high bushes.

As the summer wears on, Justin and Corey still haven't found any arrowheads, but they have improved their riding skills. The trip to the mountains is getting closer.

This summer the snow in the mountains has been slow to melt, which pushes back the date of the trip. By the time the rich mountain grass is ready for the Pitchfork herd, it is also time to harvest the ranch's hay crop. A couple of the hands are needed to bring in the hay, which means they cannot help with the cattle. More riders are needed to help drive the cattle up to the summer range.

Scott thinks both Justin and Corey can handle this work. Ray's own grandson, Jim, helped move the cattle last summer and will help out again this time. He is twelve, like Corey.

But Ray is still not sure how Justin will do. He does not want to spend valuable time watching out for the younger boy. Scott says it will be good for Justin to take part in the drive before helping out in the mountains, and both boys finally get permission to go.

After they assist Ray, Scott, and several of the other hands in moving the cattle to the mountains, the

three boys will stay up there for about two weeks—until school starts back up in August—to help Scott and Ray move the cattle around the mountain range.

The first morning of the cattle drive, Justin feels as if he has been asleep for only a few minutes when Scott and Sheila roust him and his brother out of bed for breakfast. Each morning for five days Justin and Corey saddle up early at the ranch and help to drive the cattle into the mountains, returning home at night to eat and sleep. There are about one thousand cows, each with one calf, and about forty bulls.

First the riders move all the cattle into a holding pasture halfway up the mountains. Then, four times, they separate out a few hundred and drive them up the rugged dirt trail that twists steeply up and over the first mountain crest and on toward Jack Creek. It is long and tiring work, but all the hours spent riding with their father on afternoons and weekends pay off for Justin and Corey. They've taken a big step—from watching their father work, to working at his side.

Justin stands on a mountain cliff, not too close to the edge, and feels the cool wind on his face. Before him is the Greybull Valley and the Pitchfork Ranch. He can just see his home far below him. If he had wings, he might be able to glide down easily to his front porch.

Behind Justin is the huge Shoshone National Forest. National forest land, found in many states, is also called "public land." It belongs to the American people, who can use it in many different ways, including hiking, camping, and hunting. In the West, cattle ranches pay a fee to use the public land to graze their herds. The Pitchfork Ranch has permission to use it for forty days this summer. The government's job is to watch out for the land and make sure it is not misused.

Some people think herds of cattle are bad for public land and its wildlife. They claim cattle pollute the creeks, damage creek beds, and don't leave enough for the wild animals—deer, moose, elk, bighorn sheep—to eat. Cattle that are allowed to spend too much time in one meadow will damage the vegetation.

The ranchers say that though some ranches in the past might have allowed their cattle to harm the land, today most are very careful to manage the cattle in a way that treats the land with respect. Ray and Scott will work hard for the next forty days to make sure the Pitchfork cattle are grazed properly, and that no mountain meadows are overgrazed.

<hr/>

Certain areas of the vast mountain range take their name from some of the bigger creeks. The Jack Creek area is the part of the national forest land where the Pitchfork Ranch has a grazing permit. And nestled in the pine trees right in the middle of the area—just up the hill from Jack Creek—is Jack Creek Cabin.

The Pitchfork cowboys have used the old log cabin during the summer for over sixty years. The small, one-room cabin has no electricity or plumbing, but all a summer range cowboy needs is a warm place to eat and sleep out of the mountain chill, and a corral for the horses. Water is brought from a nearby spring. Meals are cooked on a gas stove. Heat comes from a wood stove, and light from a gas lamp that hangs from the low ceiling.

"Hey, Corey," Scott says when they first get inside. "Could you turn on the light, please." Corey looks along the wall by the door, but cannot find a light switch. Everyone chuckles. Their new home takes some getting used to. The cowboys will only return to the Pitchfork once a week to bathe and get more food and supplies.

After the very hard week of driving the cattle up the mountain, it is time to settle into the cabin and begin the daily job of keeping the four different herds moving from meadow to meadow.

The day for the mountain cowboys begins before the sun rises. At 4:00 A.M. Ray begins making breakfast and Scott goes out to wrangle the horses in the nearby pasture and bring them into the corral. It is very dark, but he finds the horses easily. One horse has a bell around its neck, and all the horses tend to stay grouped close together.

Justin, Corey, and Jim are not used to getting up so early. They crawl out of their sleeping bags and pull on their boots very slowly. "Keep going! Keep moving!" Scott calls out as he puts more wood in the stove. "We've got a job to do! We're not playing!"

As Ray's cooking fills the cabin with good smells, the sleepy boys finally pull up to the table. Ray produces a stack of pancakes a foot high and a plate full of bacon. There is a cup of hot chocolate for each boy. Soon it is time to wash dishes, brush teeth, gather gear, saddle up, and ride out. It is just barely light.

Cattle are best moved early in the day because that is when they are all "mothered up." In the afternoons the mothers and calves can become separated, but at night and early in the morning they find each other again.

After doing this job for seventeen years, Ray knows when and where to move each herd, but he and Scott are glad the three boys are there to help. The cowboys ride to one of the herds each morning, round up any cattle who have strayed from the herd, and move them to another part of the mountain range. There is the constant noise of cattle complaining and riders yelling.

"HEY THERE! GET ON UP THERE!" they shout at the slower cattle to convince them to catch up with the rest of the herd. "HO! MOVE IT—MOVE IT—MOVE IT! YEE-HAW!" The cowboys slap their legs with their gloved hands and zigzag back and forth behind the herd to keep it together and moving in the right direction. They hardly ever touch the cattle.

There is very little fast riding; most of it is done at

a steady walk. The cattle and the horses can get tired out, just as people would, and there is a long way to go. Riding fast can also lead to falls. It would be very difficult and would take a long time to get an injured horse or rider off the mountain and into town for treatment.

But every once in a while a cow or a calf decides it does not want to walk with the rest of the herd. When a calf takes off at a run, Justin quickly pulls his reins to his right and spurs Brewster to head it off before it gets too far away. Working together the horse and rider turn the calf back to its mother in the herd.

At midday they leave the cattle to graze, and head back to the cabin for a rest and lunch. One day they make peanut butter sandwiches. On another day lunch is a bowl of chili from a can. They drink soft drinks kept cool in the spring, or the spring water itself, cold and delicious.

In the afternoon, after moving a herd across Jack Creek and around the other side of the canyon, the riders return to the cabin. But no matter how tired or hungry a cowboy is at the end of the day, he must first care for his horse. Justin helps to unsaddle Brewster and then fetches a bucket of oats from the feed and tack shed. When the horses are let out into the pasture, they roll and graze, glad to be free of their hot and heavy saddles.

One night at dinner as the daylight begins to fade, everyone watches as a buck deer with a large rack of horns noses around just outside the cabin. All the cowboys have often seen deer before, but this sight holds everyone spellbound. The deer finally walks around the cabin and out of sight. It is time for bed.

As the days fly by, Justin learns the names of all the other creeks in the area. There is Little Jack Creek, Willow Creek, Haymaker Creek, Webster Creek, and Red Creek. He learns the trails and how to tell when it is time to move the cattle to another mountain meadow.

The work is not physically hard on the riders, though Justin finds that riding up and down hills forces him to use his leg muscles constantly. But the job does require long hours of concentration. When Ray calls for a break in the riding, the cowboys sit around telling stories and enjoying the view of the mountains. It feels good to get off Brewster to stretch and to rest or to walk around a bit. While Brewster grazes, Justin hunts up a snack himself.

Because the morning rides are long, everyone usually puts a candy bar or an apple in a pocket for when the midmorning hungries hit. More than once, Justin is too sleepy to remember this and later has to ask someone for part of his snack. "Aw, Justin, try to remember your own candy bar tomorrow!" Corey says, laughing as he breaks his candy bar in half and tosses part over to Justin.

The mountains teem with life in the short season

between snows. Wildflowers grow everywhere in every color of the rainbow. One day the riders come across a moose and its baby. On another day Corey, with his sharp eyes, spots a coyote walking along the top of a nearby ridge. A couple of times a thunderstorm rolls across the mountains toward the riders, but they pull on the rain gear that is always tied onto the back of their saddles and keep going.

Too soon it is time to load up the four-wheel-drive pickup and bump slowly down the road back to the Pitchfork. Justin, Corey, and Jim must get ready for school, but Scott and Ray will return to Jack Creek to stay until the forty days are up. By then the first mountain snows will be coming, with cold winds whistling around the cabin at night. They will be glad when it is time to bring the cattle back down to the valley.

"Those are awful long hours in the saddle," Ray says, "but Justin did his part. He held up his share of the work."

In the days before school starts, Justin and Corey take their pigs to the county fair, where they are auctioned. Justin's pig is a champion and sells for almost five hundred dollars, which goes directly into his bank savings account.

There is little time left for exploring around the ranch. But by next summer Corey will be strong enough to open and close the fence gates, and the boys will be able to ride out by themselves. They know their parents will trust them with the horses, for they earned that trust at Jack Creek.

Next summer Justin wants to look for arrowheads again and to ride Brewster out with his brother to the abandoned bunkhouses used by the hands back in Otto Franc's day. But most of all he hopes for the chance to return to Jack Creek and be a cowboy once again.